UCHI DESHI AND THE MASTER

UCHI DESHI
and
THE MASTER

Malcolm Phipps

eMPi Publishing
23, Garland Close, Hemel Hempstead, Herts. HP2 5HU.
England

First published in 1992 by
eMPi Publishing,
23, Garland Close, Hemel Hempstead, Herts. HP2 5HU. England.
Tel. (0442) 69850

Printed by; The College of Estate Management, Whiteknights, Reading, Berks. RG6 2AW. England.
Tel. (0734) 861101

British Library Cataloguing-in-Publication Data.
A Catalogue record for this book is available from the British Library.

ISBN 0 9519835 0 4

TO MY GRANDCHILDREN

CHRISTOPHER AND SARAH-LOUISE

ACKNOWLEDGEMENTS

The Author, Illustrator and eMPi Publishing are grateful to the following people for their help in the publication of this book; Terry O'Neill 6th Dan, Editor of 'Terry O'Neill's Fighting Arts International', Nina Khanna 2nd Dan, for her tiresome work on the layout and Graphic Design and to Bill Burgar Snr. and CHAT for the invaluable use of their equipment. Finally, we would like to express our gratitude to the anonymous author of 'Footprints'.

Cover; 'Wave Of Truth' by Tracey Phipps

DISCLAIMER

CONTENTS

FOREWORD

I have known Malcolm and Tracey for many years now: their love and enthusiasm for Karate is infectious. They have developed, over the last eight years an excellent association named 'Seishinkai Shotokan Karate', one that follows strictly the traditional values of Karate-do.

Malcolm, in his 20 years of Karate, has produced not only champions at literally all levels, but more importantly, day to day students of an exceptionally high standard.

Tracey has also achieved much success over her 14 years in Karate. She has been British and English *Kumite* (sparring) champion and FEKO *Kata* (forms) champion, and has represented the country many times all over the world. Her first love though, like her husband, is traditional Karate and its many values.

• •

After such a glowing introduction you would no doubt expect a book, produced by this dynamic duo, to be of a high standard. Especially as Malcolm has recently had published his first novel, *'Wild Oats In Cornwall'*, with much success. I doubt that anyone will be disappointed with this, his second effort.

'Uchi Deshi and the Master', strikes me as one of those little gems on the art of Karate-do. Sometimes serious, sometimes light-hearted but always entertaining, these stories of a wise, old Master and his young prodigy bring home the many complex philosophies of Karate-do in a way that you will never forget them.

Tracey's input is the superb cover illustration and the numerous line drawings which bring the characters to life.

Karateka will of course love this collection of tales but then they are biased . . . I'd wager that should this little tome find its way into the hands of non-practitioners they may well be tempted to go in search of a dojo!

I enjoyed the book from start to finish and would heartily recommend it.

Terry O'Neill
6th Dan Japan Karate Association
Publisher and Editor of
'Fighting Arts International'.

1

THOSE WHO KNOW

Uchi Deshi was a young man of twenty-one years and he was absolutely elated. After a long and rigorous grading, he had just been awarded his shodan by his Sensei, a wise, old Okinawan Master.

The young man bowed deeply and thanked the Master for all his teaching and patience over the last five years.

"No thanks is needed Deshi San, you have worked hard and learnt many lessons".

"How can I ever repay you Master?"

The old man thought for a moment as he stroked his rather long and wispy grey beard. He eventually spoke.

"You will take the class for tomorrows lesson Deshi San, this will be your repayment".

"Oss! Domo arigato gozaimasu", the young man bowed deeply, turned and ran for home.

Next day the young black-belt felt a panic rising from the very pit of his stomach.

What should he teach?

What to do?

He had never stood in front of the class before. The Master had always taken the class and had covered all topics thoroughly. Should he try and copy one of the Master's many excellent classes or would this be wrong? He removed his footwear and entered the dojo.

The Master sat quietly in the small glass office situated by the entrance to the dojo.

With a wave of his hand he gestured for the new black-belt to carry on.

The students were all busily warming up. Some were thudding home well-distanced punches on the many makiwara situated around the dojo walls, others were busy stretching.

It was now or never.

"Two lines!" The dojo captain shouted after receiving the nod from the new shodan.

All was ready. The silence was unnerving. Panic set in deeper.

"Does everyone know what I am going to teach today?" He enquired of the expectant class.

"No sensei", they shook their heads in unison.

"Well then, there seems little point in carrying on!" And with this remark bowed deeply and left the dojo.

The Master caught him up quickly.

"That was a disgrace Deshi San, whatever were you doing?"

"My humble apologies Master".

"For punishment you will take tomorrows lesson instead, now be on your way and prepare".

"Oss! Master".

The next day arrived all too quickly. The same panic had set in. He found himself stood once again in front of a now very expectant class.

"Does everyone know what I shall be teaching today?" The students were now wary to this and as one body all nodded in total unison,

"Yes sensei".

"Well if you already know, there seems little point in carrying on!" And with this remark the young man turned and departed quickly from the dojo.

Again the Master caught him up after a few yards.

"Whatever do you think you are doing Deshi San? That was another total disgrace".

"Oss! Master, again I am so sorry", his head was bowed as he gazed down at his zori.

"Well Deshi San you will take tomorrows lesson as a punishment, and you will carry on taking the lessons until you get it right, understand?"

"Oss! Master", and with this he bowed once more and made for home and safety.

After a sleepless night the next day dawned all too quickly.

He was still not totally prepared. Whatever would he teach?

The scenario was now a familiar one. He was stood in front of the huge expectant class, the Master quietly watching from his glass office.

"Does everyone know what I shall teach today?" He once again asked of the class.

The class were totally confused, a few even cringed.

Some shook their heads, "No sensei", and some nodded in the affirmative, "Yes sensei".

There was an uneasy silence.

"Good! Well all those who know, can teach those that don't know!"

And with this seemingly daring and stupid remark and a quick bow, he made for the dojo door.

The old Master caught him this time before he could leave.

The young shodan panicked.

"Sorry Master, I am a failure to you".

"What do you mean Deshi San? That is one of the best lessons I have ever witnessed!"

"How do you mean Master?"

"ALL THOSE WHO KNOW, SHOULD TEACH THOSE THAT DO NOT KNOW! This is indeed an important lesson Deshi San in the art of karate-do.

One should always be ready to help others no matter what their rank or status. Well done, you will make a fine black-belt".

"Oss! Master and thank you, for the lesson really came from you".

The old man smiled, "Oss! Deshi San, now be on your way".

"One step at a time is the key"

2

ONE STEP AT A TIME

*I*t was a couple of months since Uchi Deshi's shodan grading when he approached the Master, with what seemed to him an extremely important question.
"How long do I have to wait Master before I am allowed to take the nidan exam?"
"How long is a piece of bamboo Deshi San?"
He thought hard for a couple of seconds, a puzzled look on his face.
"There is no answer Master".
"Exactly Deshi San, same with nidan exam. After two years hard training we will evaluate the situation".
"That seems a long time Master?"
"What is the rush Deshi San, do not try to run before you can walk. One step at a time is the key to good karate progression. Come into my office and sit down".
Uchi Deshi obeyed and now sat opposite the Master. Only an old wooden desk stood between them.
"The following analogy may help you understand more what I am trying to tell you. Imagine it is night-time. There is no moon and it is pitch black. You cannot see

a hand in front of your face. You are stood on the bank of a deep and wide river that has to be crossed. There is a fearful current, so swimming is out. There are no bridges for miles in either direction.

There is though, a single line of small stepping-stones, neatly spaced reaching to the other side and safety. You must get across! Your life depends on it! You are armed only with a torch. You proceed. Now you must ask yourself three questions Deshi San. Do you shine the torch on your destination, the other side of the river? Do you shine it a few stones ahead all the time? Or do you shine it only on the next stone, first making sure you are safely stood on the stone you now occupy?

The answer I hope Deshi San is obvious, yes?"

"Yes I see Master, the stones could be construed as the different belts and grades in our karate life?"

"Indeed Deshi San that is part of the story, but do not forget the torch, this is of huge importance as it is 'The Do or Way'. Do not be in a rush to get grades and belts. These are of little consequence. It is what you can do that matters not the colour or title of your grade. I wonder how many people throughout the world would be training in the art of karate if there were no competitions or coloured belts to be won, as in the days of the great Okinawan Masters such as Funakoshi. This would certainly sort out the chaff from the wheat".

"Yes Master I understand, but I know the nidan syllabus reasonably well already".

"You know it in a very shallow sense Deshi San. The kihon, kata and kumite contained therein need years of practice before they can be mastered. You must practice them everyday for at least two years. Remember, the drop of water wears the stone hollow, not by force but by persistence".

"Oss Master! I understand".

"Good Deshi San I hope so. Enjoy your everyday karate training, the future will look after itself. Remember Funakoshi's famous words, 'The ultimate aim of the art of karate lies not in victory or defeat but in the perfection of the character of its participants'. Now go and put this into practice Deshi San, for it takes a lifetime to perfect one's character, not a few months".

"Oss, thank you Master, I will remember what you have told me today".

With this he stood, bowed deeply and left for home.

"The mountain does not laugh at the river because it is lowly , nor does   the river speak ill of the mountain because it cannot move"

3

A FIGHT TO THE DEATH

The hours lesson had been all sparring. Uchi Deshi the young shodan had not been beaten once. In fact he had not been beaten now by anyone for over a month. The students were all busy showering and changing in the small room at the far end of the dojo, sweaty and tired after the extremely tough lesson and the ritual cleaning of the dojo floor.

"There is no-one in the dojo I cannot beat!" Uchi Deshi talked excitedly to his friend, a young brown-belt.

"No I know Sensei, you are very good indeed".

Uchi Deshi smiled a somewhat, 'Yes I know how good I am smile', as he patted his friend on the back.

"Look around Deshi San, there is someone here you have yet to beat", a voice boomed from the doorway.

The Master had been listening outside the paper-thin door.

Uchi Deshi bowed deeply and began looking quickly from side to side.

· "I see no-one Master?"

"Look harder!"

He looked.

"Only you Master and I know I cannot defeat you".

"Not me Deshi San - please look harder".

"I am sorry Master, I have beaten everyone in here many times", Uchi Deshi was reasonably confident of his reply.

"Close your eyes Deshi San and keep them tightly shut. Take my hand and follow me. I will stand you in front of the one student you have not yet beaten. When you open your eyes you will fight this student to the death!"

The Master guided the now not-so-cocky shodan to a far wall.

Uchi Deshi started to tremble.

"Now open your eyes Deshi San".

He obeyed and found himself facing a large steamed-up mirror.

"I do not understand Master?"

"Wipe the mist from the mirror Deshi San".

He quickly obeyed.

"Now do you see him? You are looking at the one person in the dojo you have never beaten - Yourself! You are still swollen with a false pride Deshi San and therefore have not mastered yourself from within".

"Oss! Master, what must I do?"

"Do not be boastful about who you can or cannot beat. The true martial artist is humble, never speaking of such things. As with the mirror Deshi San, wipe the mist from your eyes so as to see yourself and others more clearly. Everyone in the Universe has a purpose - The mountain does not laugh at the river because it is lowly, nor does the river speak ill of the mountain because it cannot move".

Uchi Deshi bowed deeply.

"Oss! And thank you for the lesson Master".

"Oss! Never forget this day, for it is an extremely important one in your long journey".

"Oss! Master, I will remember". He gave one final bow and departed.

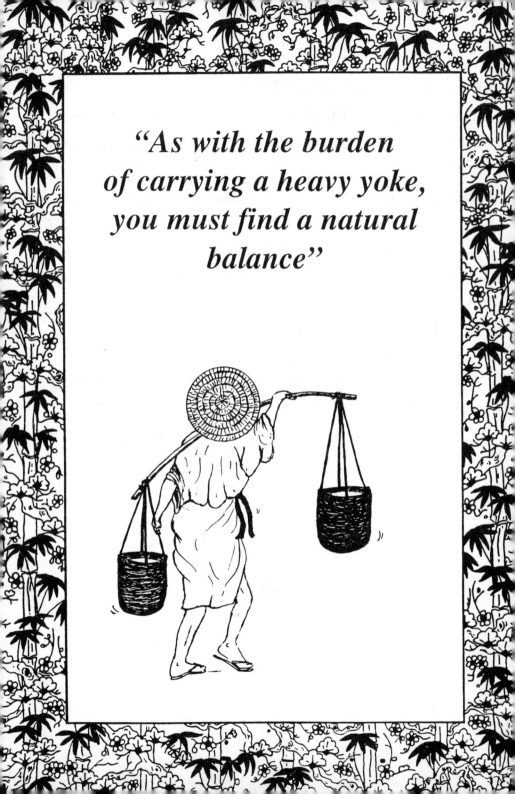

4

THE COMPETITION

*U*chi Deshi had now been a shodan for nearly a year. His progress had been slow but precise under the watchful eye of his wise Master.

The town he lived in was holding its annual karate tournament at the local sports hall in just over a months time.

"Should I enter this year Master?"

"What do you think Deshi San?"

"I feel it is expected of me Master, now I am a black-belt".

"Nothing is expected of you Deshi San, only what you come to expect from yourself, therefore the decision must be yours".

"Then I shall enter the kata event".

"No Deshi San, you must enter both kumite and kata if you are going to compete at all".

"Why Master?"

"It is not good to just excel in one part of karate, whether it be in the dojo or on the competition floor. If you enter, then enter both. Always seek a balance. As with the burden of carrying a heavy yoke, you must find a natural balance Deshi San".

"But I do not feel that confident in the kumite section Master?"

"Then do not enter at all Deshi San. Wait until you are fully prepared to enter both. In order to conquer others, first you must conquer yourself".

"Oss Master".

"Go away and think hard about this competition Deshi San".

With another bow Uchi Deshi quietly left the dojo.

Uchi Deshi thought long and hard for many days and many sleepless nights. Eventually his pride got the better of him.

"I will enter both", he thought positively to himself.

The day of the competition arrived and Uchi Deshi was nervous. His stomach kept telling him so on his many trips to the toilet. Now inside the hall he padded up and down awaiting his name on the tannoy system. It was kata first and there were to be three rounds. All entrants performed one kata and the top eight went through into the next round to perform a second kata. From these eight entrants four would go through to the finals in the evening.

"U. DESHI!" The tannoy rang his name around the large hall.

He made his way cautiously but smartly to the arena. Now stood in the centre of the marked area, the chief referee enquired,

"Tokui kata?"

"Bassai Dai! Sensei".

"Oss!" The chief referee nodded for him to proceed. The kata was over in a flash. Uchi Deshi could not really remember performing any of the individual movements, it was all a blur and over so fast.

"Hantei!" The chief referee shouted as he blew a blast on his whistle calling for the other four judges to show their score-cards.

The judges lifted their arms in unison.

"5.4, 5.5, 5.6, 5.5, 5.5", the tannoy system informed everyone of his marks.

His score was quite average.

Half an hour later and with the first round now finished he found out just how average.

To his dismay he had not made the last eight.

He bowed and made for the toilets.

Inwardly he was not amused. Now it was all on the kumite.

This too was a non-event. He was well-beaten in the first round by a young member of the National team. Again he bowed and made for the solace of the toilets.

Twenty yards from the safety and comfort of the mens washroom he was stopped by his Master who had seen everything from a secluded position in the audience.

"Why so glum Deshi San?" He smiled.

"I was awful Master. I have let you and the dojo down".

"Why Deshi San?"

"I was knocked out in the first round of both events Master".

"Deshi San you must understand that it is the entering that is important not the winning. Competition is only a game for points and prizes, your dojo karate is of much more value. This is for enlightenment and perfection of character".

"Oss Master, you make it sound as though competition is of no importance whatsoever?"

"No Deshi San that is not what I meant. It is good for

young men and women to satisfy their ego's and their competitive urges. Since time began, humans have always competed in one form or another, whether it be for food, territory, a partner, or for some other reason. What I am saying is that karate-do is much more important than karate competition. In competition karate there is only one winner. In karate-do all are winners. In competition karate only the winners are truly fulfilled but in karate-do all are fulfilled if they follow 'The Way' properly. The real competition Deshi San is with yourself!"

"Oss! And thank you Master. I will do better next time".

"I am sure you will Deshi San especially if you remember what I have just told you. Good thing about getting knocked out in the first round this time, is it can only get better next time", he smiled a faintly wicked smile and continued, "Good-night and be in the dojo early tomorrow".

"Yes Master", Uchi Deshi bowed and made for home.

*"Uchi Deshi was to find,
that the missing piece
was of extreme
significance"*

5

THE PUZZLE

The lesson had been another hard one. Uchi Deshi, along with the other thirty or so students, was absolutely shattered and longed for a hot shower and a cool drink. The Master had pushed them to their limit.

"That was a tough one", Uchi Deshi's friend a young brown-belt sighed as they made for the changing rooms and the showers.

"I agree", he placed his hand on his friend's damp shoulder,

"I see Katsugi San is not here again?"

"No, I haven't seen him for a few weeks now. Do you think he has given up?" The brown-belt enquired.

"Probably", Uchi Deshi shrugged his shoulders, "Couldn't stand the pace".

The Master had made the last months training extremely tough, constantly forging and testing the student's spirits, through extreme hard-work and discipline.

"Must be stupid to pack up at first kyu level", the brown-belt carried on the conversation.

"He is of no importance to the class if he cannot be

bothered to turn up to the lessons".

"Not absolutely correct, Deshi San", the Master's voice broke into the dojo gossip.

"But surely Master, only those who turn up to your lesson's are of any real importance?"

"You think so Deshi San. Then come to my office after you have showered".

"Oss, Master", Uchi Deshi bowed.

The hot shower and cool can of drink had been wonderful. He felt a new man as he entered the Master's office.

"Ah, Deshi San. I want you to take this jigsaw puzzle home and complete it this evening".

The Master handed him a large cardboard box.

"Why a jigsaw puzzle Master, surely these are for children?"

"Not necessarily so", the Master shook his head. "From this puzzle you will learn an important lesson. The puzzle's picture is of a famous Karate Master. You must tell me in the morning who this Master is and what technique he is performing, understand Deshi San?"

"Oss, Master, but could I possibly do it tomorrow

evening as I was going out this evening with my friends?"
"Do not go out until you have finished the puzzle Deshi San".
"Oss!" He bowed deeply and left.

At home, in the safety and warmth of his living room, he cleared a large table and proceeded to do the puzzle. There were around 200 pieces to the jigsaw and these were now spread over the surface of the table. He slowly built up the outside square of the puzzle and worked his way carefully in. Two hours later and the final picture was nearly complete. As he neared the finish he could easily see that the picture was of a karateka performing gyakuzuki, but who?

To his total annoyance he could not find the last piece of the puzzle anywhere. He searched high and low, under the table and on the table. He shook the box the puzzle had come in vigorously and then searched and shook his holdall. Nothing. Not a sign of the final piece. The most irritating part was, the piece that was missing made up the famous karateka's face.

"Damn!" He kicked the leg of the table on his way out of the room.

He would have to tell the Master that either a piece had been missing when he was given the puzzle, or that he had lost the piece in question somewhere. Should he guess who the karateka in the picture was and hand back the jigsaw puzzle to the Master, and not say anything? It looked a little like the great Nakayama Sensei or could it be Nishiyama Sensei? Damn! No, he decided, this was not the way. It was deceitful. He must tell the truth.

Next day and now back in the Master's office, Uchi Deshi explained about the missing piece.
"So what have you learnt Deshi San?"
"Always count the pieces first, Master?"
"No, no", the Master smiled, "That is not what I meant, but perhaps a good idea all the same. Which piece is now the most important piece Deshi San?"
"The missing piece Master".
"Ah, at last Deshi San, correct. What does this convey to you about our karate class?"
He pondered for a while and eventually confessed, "I am sorry Master, I still do not see a connection?"
"Well, like the missing piece in the jigsaw puzzle, the missing student is of extreme significance. He has

attained a reasonably high level in the art of karate-do and it is of great concern that he is missing".

"But you can only work with those students who turn up to your classes Master?"

"True Deshi San, but it is imperative to find out why our friend is not here. Has something or someone upset him? Has he not understood something? Is he ill or injured? Is his family alright? At this moment in time Deshi San, like the missing piece in the puzzle, he is of great consequence and will remain so until he turns up, like the missing piece".

The Master held high the final piece of the jigsaw and smiled.

"Do you see now, Deshi San?"

"Yes Master I understand. I will call on him on my way home".

"Good, that is the correct procedure for a true karateka to take. Pass on this lesson to your brown-belt friend, so he too may understand. Never gossip Deshi San, never become Kuchi Bushi!"

"What is that Master?"

"Kuchi Bushi means 'Mouth Warrior'. This is title for gossips and people who only talk about karate, never

actually attaining anything of real importance themselves. They only have inspection not introspection.
These students are as common as grains of sand on a
beach".

"Oss, Master and thank you for such an important lesson.
By the way Master, who was the person in the picture?"

"It is of little significance Deshi San".

Uchi Deshi's eyes looked hard at the missing piece, now
lying on the table. It looked remarkably like his own
Master but he didn't have the courage to ask.

Instead he bowed deeply and left the office to train.

❀

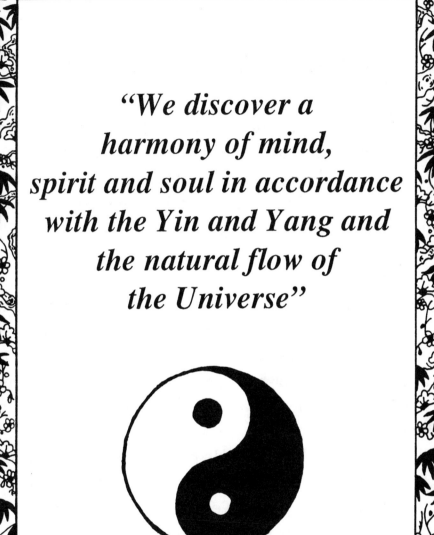

"We discover a harmony of mind, spirit and soul in accordance with the Yin and Yang and the natural flow of the Universe"

6

SUMMER GASSHUKU

*I*t was mid-summer and it was hot, very hot. The forest was green and lush and the sound of the birds was the only sound you could hear for miles. The class stood patiently in a clearing somewhere in the centre of the vast forest, awaiting the Master's next instruction.

It was the summer gasshuku, an annual event organised by the Master each July. The students would train and literally live off the land for two long weekends each year, one in the middle of summer, the other in mid-winter. The Master had carefully explained that there was nothing better for the character and comradeship than the gasshuku.
"Partner-up for Kumite!" He powerfully commanded. The thirty or so students all found themselves a partner and quickly formed two lines on their seniors. "Right, now change partners", the Master smiled, noticing that nearly everyone had partnered their best friends. "You will not learn very much if you keep on partnering your friend. A student needs to feel challenged, not

comfortable, if he or she is to better themselves".

"Oss!" The class promptly complied.

"This side, step back hidari gedan-barai, Kamaite!" The Master gestured with his hand.

The class obeyed immediately.

"Sanbon kumite, begin".

"Jodan!" The attackers shouted, nearly as one.

They moved fluently, even on the rough terrain, as they delivered their three vigorous attacks.

On the third defence, a piercing kiai made the birds in the trees move swiftly to a safer distance.

The defenders now became the attackers.

"Jodan!" They also moved powerfully against their opponent's.

On the third attack Uchi Deshi stumbled badly on a large twig and lost his balance. His partner luckily enough had good control and stopped his blow an inch from Uchi Deshi's throat.

"Hiieeee!" His opponent's fierce kiai accompanied the telling strike.

Uchi Deshi regained his composure and shook his now painful ankle. He grinned at his opponent who in turn smiled back. Smiles turned into chuckles as both could see the funny side of the incident.

"What is the joke?" The Master was now by their side.

"I stumbled on a branch Master".

"What is so funny about that Deshi San?"

"Er, I do not really know Master", he felt extremely awkward and somewhat stupid.

"Your mistake could have cost you your life in real combat. It is certainly no laughing matter, understand?" They bowed and 'oss-ed' as one.

"There is an important lesson to be learnt here. Class gather round".

The class obeyed immediately and formed a tight circle around their Master.

"If we learn nothing else on the gasshuku, so be it. What I now have to say is of extreme importance".

The class listened intently to their Master and again the only sound to be heard was that of the birds and insects.

"When you make a mistake, as our two friend's here have made", he pointed in their general direction, "Do not laugh, it is a sign of weakness. The human animal is the only animal that laughs at its own mistakes. All other animals learn immediately from their shortcomings, they do not find them in the least bit funny. We must learn from the animal kingdom, as our fathers before us and their forefathers before them and indeed the founders of the martial arts did all those many years ago. Many styles and movements in the martial arts come from the animal kingdom".

The class was now completely engrossed as the Master proceeded.

"As with the animals the karateka should be at one with the Universe. Development of our minds can only be achieved when the body has been disciplined. To attain this state we should try to imitate God's creatures. All creatures whether great or small are at one with nature. We must have the wisdom to learn their many qualities. From the Crane we learn poise, posture and self-control and from the Snake suppleness and rhythmic endurance. We can observe perfect tai-sabaki from the Mongoose, whilst the Praying Mantis teaches us composure and speed. The Tiger teaches us tenacity, forcefulness and power and the Falcon a supreme patience and near perfect kime. In nature no two elements are in conflict, therefore if we follow the ways of nature, we remove conflict from within ourselves. We discover a harmony of mind, spirit and soul in accordance with the Yin and

Yang and the natural flow of the Universe".

The class sat open-mouthed.

"Now do you understand Deshi San? It is wrong to laugh at one's mistakes. Learn not laugh! Now partner-up again".

"Oss Master!" He bowed with deep respect.

He inwardly knew that he had just learnt a very meaningful lesson. One that would stay with him for the rest of his life.

❉

"*It is like playing the flute.
Anyone can blow and
make a noise,
but to play it properly you
also have to use your fingers*"

7

THE COURSE

*T*he students were lined-up and ready for action. The whole dojo was in a state of apprehension as they awaited the arrival on the dojo floor of their Master and his honoured guest. The Course had been planned for months now and everyone had buzzed with much expectancy from the very moment they heard that the great man was coming. The guest was the legendary head of the Japanese Karate Association, the great Masatoshi Nakayama himself. Although younger than their own Master, Nakayama Shihan had trained for a longer period of time and since the death of Gichin Funakoshi had been highly instrumental in promoting karate throughout the world.

He entered the dojo with their own Master in close attendance, both men taking up position at the front of the class. The class bowed to the shrine of Funakoshi and then to the great man knelt in front of them. He arose and to Uchi Deshi's great surprise pointed to him to take the exercise routine. He bowed reverently and proceeded to the front of the dojo. He nervously took the class through a basic exercise routine, wishing sincerely that the dojo floor would open up and swallow him. He was very proud but extremely nervous. He eventually handed back to the great man with a huge sense of relief, a weight now lifted from his young shoulders.

The Course was absolutely magnificent. The students had been pushed hard physically, but in some ways even harder mentally. There seemed so much to remember. The great man had departed bodily from the dojo but his spirit lived on. Surely the sign of a truly remarkable man.

Next day the dojo was packed, students wanting to put in to practice the previous days teaching.
Uchi Deshi cornered the Master as he entered his office.
"What did Master Nakayama mean when he said, 'We must all work EVEN MORE on our hips', Master?"
"It is true Deshi San. As you well know all karate comes from the hips. Our kicks, blocks and punches should all incorporate the correct use of koshi. Many students throughout the world just use brute force when they strike or block, without ever really understanding the

correct use of the hips. It is like playing the flute".

"How so Master?"

"Well anyone can blow and make a noise, but to play it properly you also have to use your fingers. In our case, our hips. Now do you see?"

"Oss Master!"

"Did you enjoy the Course Deshi San?"

"It was superb Master, he is indeed a great man".

"Yes indeed he is. Do not forget what he taught you yesterday".

"No, I will not Master".

"A good Course should be enjoyed three times Deshi San".

"Three times - how Master?"

"The anticipation, the participation and the remembrance".

"Oss! I see what you mean Master, thank you".

"Good Deshi San. Now go and warm-up ready for today's lesson".

He bowed once more, feeling one step closer to enlightenment as he left the Master's office.

"Dojo no soji"

8

THE THREE SIGHTS

The days lesson was coming to an end. The Master had given the senior class two hours instruction on the kata Hangetsu and they were now feeling extremely exhausted.

"Arms slowly up and breathe in deeply through your nose", the class silently obeyed lifting their weary arms above their heads.

"And now slowly exhaling through your mouth, bring your arms down to your sides".

The class repeated the exercise five times.

Uchi Deshi felt much better now, mentally and physically revived.

"Gather round in a small circle and sit down for today's philosophical lesson", the Master gestured for the class to obey his command.

They gathered round him like expectant children waiting to hear their favourite story.

"Deshi San", the Master looked him in the eyes, "Which is the most important day in your life?"

Uchi Deshi thought for a moment.

"The day I received my black-belt from you Master", he confidently replied, "I will never forget that day".

"Good, I am glad to hear it".

"And you Saito San, what day is to be your most momentous?" The Master now directed his question to a young eighteen year old brown-belt.

Noritaka Saito quickly replied,

"The day I pass and receive my black-belt from you Master".

He rather liked the way the Master had received Uchi Deshi's answer and was reasonably confident he would also get a satisfactory pat on the back.

"Mmmm", the Master looked at them both stroking his grey beard,

"Both answers are wrong!"

Noritaka Saito and Uchi Deshi looked quickly in each others direction. It was the classes turn to look smug. The Master on seeing this then asked the whole class,

"What then is your most important day?" He asked them all in general.

"The day we were born, Master?"

"The day we first started karate training, Master?"

"When we left school and got jobs, Master?"

"The day we get married, Master?"

"The day when we have our own children, Master?"

"O.K. Stop!" He lifted his hands for them to obey, a smile appearing on his lips.

"These are all good answers but not the one I am looking for".

He looked at them all in a fatherly fashion.

"The most important day of your lives, is TODAY!"

The class sent quick and furtive looks to each other, not quite understanding the Master's drift. What was so good about today? Had they missed something?

He read their thoughts.

"There are three sights. Firstly, we have hindsight. It is good to have memories, some good and some bad, but we must not live in the past. It is gone, there is nothing we can do about it. We cannot have those times again. Secondly, we have foresight. It is also good to have plans and dreams, but we must not live in the future. Nobody knows what is in store for us. We may not be here tomorrow. So this too is a waste of time.

Finally, we have insight. We must learn to live for the moment, for in all truthfulness it is all we have.

The past is gone. The future may not happen, so it is for

today we must live. Enjoy every minute, for time itself cannot be regained. It is a most precious commodity. So live not for tomorrow, or for yesterday, but for today, do you all understand?"

"Oss Master", the class spoke as one with true sincerity, for they all knew in their hearts that they had just learnt a very powerful lesson.

"Good, now get the cleaning cloths and purify the dojo floor".

They arose and made for the small cupboard next to the Master's office. A bucket was filled with disinfected warm water and the cloths dampened. The class stood in a line at one end of the dojo and on the command of the dojo captain, "Hajime!" All ran back in unison, cloths pressed firmly against the floor.

"You see", shouted the Master, "It is a little like cleaning the dojo floor. The most important piece is the piece you are actually cleaning, not the parts you have gone past or not yet reached. If you do this properly you will have no need to worry, for the job will have been done correctly in the first place", he strode towards his office,

"Deshi San, you have missed a bit. Look, there!" He pointed, a wry smile appearing on his wise old face.

❧

"Only one
set of
footprints -

could be
seen"

9

THE DREAM

*U*chi Deshi had had a terrible night. He had tossed and turned in the heat, sweat streaming from his brow. Again the same dream.

This had to be the third or fourth time, each time exactly the same.

He was walking along a deserted beach with the Master. In front of them and in the sky passed Uchi Deshi's past life. Behind them all that could be seen were their footprint's. The soothing sound of the sea was the only sound to be heard. Neither man spoke. Uchi Deshi could not help noticing that every time something horrible or troublesome happened in his life, only one set of footprints could be seen. When everything returned rosy and going to plan both sets of footprints would return.

Why did the Master keep deserting him at these times of need?

He awoke again kicking off the thin sheet that half-covered his damp body. He must ask the Master if he knew the meaning of this dream, it was now starting to haunt him.

Next day he arrived early at the dojo. The Master sat quietly in his office reading an old book. It was the Master's pride and joy as not many copies could now be found. It was Gichin Funakoshi's 'Ryukyu Kempo Karate' and Master Funakoshi had personally signed the Master's copy and placed a small message on the first page. It read, 'Shoshin o wasurezu', (Do not forget the spirit and humility of a beginner).

The Master looked up as the door opened, following the customary knock.

"Yes Deshi San, how may I help you?"

Uchi Deshi bowed and stumbled his way through his opening words,

"I do not know how to explain Master, it is rather awkward".

"Well sit down, relax and start from the beginning".

Uchi Deshi obeyed.

"Well Master, I have been having this recurring dream and it has been bothering me. Each time I awake with a start, sweating profusely. I feel a little silly Master coming to you with my dreams".

"Do not underestimate the power of dreams Deshi San. Please continue".

Uchi Deshi told the story of the dream to the Master in every detail, leaving nothing to chance.

When he eventually finished he felt a load lift from his young shoulders.

"That is it Master".

"I see", the Master was now in deep contemplation. Eventually he spoke,

"Yes, I know the meaning of this dream Deshi San".

"You do Master?" Uchi Deshi felt a sudden surge of relief.

"I will explain. In your dream, when things were going well, I was always with you, yes?"

"Yes Master, two sets of footprints".

"And when things got rough in your life, only one set of footprints could be seen, true?"

"Yes, that is it Master".

"It was then, in those troubled times Deshi San when I carried you. That was the reason for only one set of footprints".

Uchi Deshi sat flabbergasted.

All had been revealed by this great man. A tear welled-up in his eyes for he knew this to be true.

"I do not know what to say Master, except thank you".

"The only thanks needed Deshi San is that you train hard, always have respect and loyalty for your elders and pass on 'The Way' to others you touch on your journey through life".

"Thank you Master, I will".

He left the Master's office, not for the first time a wiser and better man.

✻

"Karate ni sente nashi"

10

THE FIGHT

*U*chi Deshi and his two friends were on their way home after another hard lesson. They had been taught kata Gankaku for the whole hour and their legs ached. The Master had had them standing on one leg in migi and hidari ashi-dachi for a long time, to improve and test their balance.

The small party talked excitedly about the kata. They were three young shodans, all in their early twenties and had been friends for many years, having been at school together from the age of five.

They rounded a corner into a small side-street, now only half a mile from their homes. A gang of five young men and a girl had followed them from the dojo and were now taunting them from a nearby alley-way.

"Yaaaa! Ichi, Ni, San, Yaaaa! Karate is for weird-do's!" Uchi Deshi and his friends took no notice.

This prompted the loudmouth of the group even more. "Who's just scrubbed the dojo floor then? Karateka are a load of old washerwomen, Yaaaa! Heeeeyaaaaah!" The young man did a bad impression of the late Bruce

Lee.

Still the group of karateka took no notice.

The local thugs drew closer, their bravery growing with every second. One of them threw a dummy kick in Uchi Deshi's direction and he quickly felt himself tighten-up, ready for action. His zanshin was at its highest peak. The adrenalin now racing throughout his young body made him feel strangely quite sick.

"Oooooh, hard-man are we?" The kicker taunted more.

"Please leave us alone. We are not harming you, we just wish to go to our homes peacefully", one of the other young black-belts intervened.

"Get lost!" The thug pushed the speaker on the shoulder.

"Please do not do that", the shodan asked politely, regaining his posture.

"I said they were a load of old washerwomen didn't I?" The loudmouth laughed to his friends.

"Got any cigarettes?" Loudmouth's derision was now re-directed at Uchi Deshi.

"I am sorry we do not smoke".

"Oh no, of course not, little goody karateka don't smoke do they?"

"One or two do", the third black-belt spoke for the first

time.

"Who asked you?" Loudmouth's aggression was now getting out of hand as he pushed the shodan in the chest.

"Leave him alone, he has done you no harm", Uchi Deshi's voice had a slight quiver in its tone.

"Shut it! Big mouth", the trouble-maker made a grab for Uchi Deshi's thin shirt.

Before the man could make a successful grab, Uchi Deshi had hit him with a low, powerful mae-geri straight into his testicles.

The thug doubled-up in pain.

"You lousy ....! I'll have you for that", he made a half-hearted attempt to punch Uchi Deshi.

Uchi Deshi side-stepped successfully and unleashed a powerful jodan mawashi-geri which hit the man square on the cheekbone. He dropped to the floor like a sack of potatoes, totally unconscious.

The rest of the group now looked a little half-hearted, seeing their mate completely motionless on the rough ground.

One, a little braver than the rest took off his leather belt. The buckle was huge as he swished it at one of the other shodan's heads. The black-belt ducked and in the same action went headlong into the man before he had time to arrest the swing. His left hand quickly held the offending arm across the attacker's own body and with his right arm produced a quick and dynamic mawashi-empi-uchi. The elbow hit the man square in the face and was accompanied by a cracking sound as his nose splattered across his face.

He dropped on to one knee holding his face in his hands and moaning.

The other gang members, on witnessing this horrific and humiliating spectacle had taken to their heels.

"I think we had better call for an ambulance?" The third black-belt spoke anxiously.

"Good idea, you go and we will stay with these", Uchi Deshi pointed toward an empty phone booth on the corner of the street.

Eventually the ambulance arrived and took the two thugs to the local hospital. Neither were as badly hurt as first it had seemed. One had sustained a badly broken nose, the other had had his jaw bone unhinged and was suffering from mild concussion. Their 'brave' so-called friends had disappeared into thin

60

air.

Next day at the dojo Uchi Deshi explained to the Master the happenings of the previous day.

"Yes, I have already heard".

"You have Master?"

"Yes, from the hospital. I hope you will be glad to know they are both in reasonably good health and will be released in a few days?"

"Oss Master, that is good. Were we wrong to hit them with such force Master?"

"Did you provoke the attack Deshi San?"

"Certainly not Master. You have taught us many times the principal of 'Karate ni sente nashi', (There is no first attack in karate)".

"Then by all accounts I think you did extremely well Deshi San, but do not let this shroud your judgement for the future. Karate must always and only be used as a last method of defence".

"Oss! Have you ever had to use your karate Master?"

"I will never tell you Deshi San, for it is not for boasting. The true test of your character starts now. Tell no-one. Remember the adage, 'Donkeys you can tell by their big ears, fools by their big mouths'. It is now time for silence Deshi San. If you can master your tongue in this matter, then you will have done everything correctly".

"Oss", he bowed, "I will Master, but what about the others?"

"I have already spoken with them. They have given me their promise also. The honour of our dojo is in your young hands".

"We will not let you down Master".

He bowed once more and left the office to train.

"*An extinct volcano is just another miserable mountain*"

11

SPIRIT OF THE VOLCANO

*T*he lesson had seemed twice as long as normal. The day was an extremely humid one and the students were tired and drenched in sweat. Still the Master insisted on more spirit.

"You have fifteen more minutes to train, push yourselves hard, do not let your tiredness get the better of you".

"Oss Master!" The class shouted as one.

Uchi Deshi felt like fainting. He had never worked so hard in his young life.

"Stepping forwards fast speed, mae-geri, mawashi-geri, uraken-uchi, gyakuzuki, understand?"

"Oss Master!"

"Hajime!"

The class started off in unison with good intent, but many students were now feeling the pressure and their technique and spirit were at a low ebb.

"Yame!" The Master shouted from his position at the front of the class, "Gather round and listen well".

"Oss!" The students obeyed immediately, glad of the

welcome rest.

"You must always train with spirit, even when tired. Do not let your body dictate to your mind. Karateka must overcome this weakness and push themselves till they can honestly go no further. Please remember, 'An extinct volcano is just another miserable mountain'. Ask yourself the question, are you an extinct volcano or an active one? Both look the same from the outside, but inside one is dead, whilst the other is smouldering waiting to explode. Karate demands a strong spirit, ne?"

"Oss Master", the class nodded their immediate reply.

"Good, then up on your feet and let's finish todays lesson with good spirit".

The class rose and moved quickly back to their places in the dojo.

"Right, as before. Mae-geri, mawashi-geri, uraken-uchi, gyakuzuki, fast speed!"

"Oss!"

For the next ten minutes most of the class gave it all they could, but there were one or two who had not listened to the Master's earlier address. He instructed these guilty students to stay behind and clean the dojo floor. The others, whose spirit was strong right to the very end, would be excused this chore today.

The class, now over, formed its customary two lines in seiza facing the shrine, the Master at the front. Uchi Deshi was dojo captain for the day and began the chant of the dojo kun,
"Hitotsu! Jinkaku Kansei Ni Tsutomuru Koto!"
The class followed the chant promising to strive for perfection of character.
"Hitotsu! Makoto No Michi O Mamoru Koto!"
His voice rang out a second time.
Again the class followed his lead, vowing to defend the paths of truth.
"Hitotsu! Doryoku No Seishin O Yashinau Koto!"
This time their pledge was to foster the spirit of effort.
"Hitotsu! Reigi O Omonzuru Koto!"
The class again followed the dojo captain giving their word to honour the principles of etiquette.
"Hitotsu! Kekki No Yu O Imashimuru Koto!"
The final line vowed to guard against impetuous courage.

"Mokuso", the Master's voice followed the kun almost immediately.

The students all closed their eyes and their breathing became more relaxed.

"Think on the third line of the kun today. You promised to foster the spirit of effort. Therefore obey your vows at all times, even when the body is weak and the spirit wanes".

The class remained silent, now deeply meditating on the Master's instructions.

After about a minute the Master's voice broke the appealing silence,

"Mokuso, yame!"

The students all opened their eyes, their breathing now more tranquil.

"Domo arigato gozaimasu", the Master bowed to the class.

They courteously returned the gesture.

The Master then turned to face the dojo shrine. A large picture of Master Funakoshi looked down upon the class.

"Shihan ni rei!" Uchi Deshi's voice instructed the class to bow in remembrance of Master Funakoshi.

The Master then turned back to face the class.

"Sensei ni rei!" This time the bow was to their own teacher, who in turn returned the bow. For the purpose of the bowing ceremony at the beginning and end of every lesson, the Master had insisted on being called 'Sensei' and not 'Shihan', in respect and in gratitude to Master Gichin Funakoshi, the founder.

He had expounded many times that if it were not for this great man, many people in the world would not be practising the art of karate-do.

"It is of great importance to know what this man gave up for you and I", the Master had given this lecture many times, instructing all of the students to read Master Funakoshi's many books, especially, 'Karate-do - My Way of Life'.

"Reading these books will give you a deeper insight into the way of karate and what Master Funakoshi tried, and indeed succeeded in achieving. He was truly a great man".

The class agreed by the customary 'oss' and polite nod of the head.

"The sensible ones among you will now go out and obtain a copy and read. The not so sensible will ignore my wise advice totally. This is often the way of the young".

"Master, I have read all of the Master's works that are readily available, what should I now read?" A young black-belt seemed to be slightly showing-off.

"Read them all again. I guarantee that each time you pick up one of the Master's books, you will learn something anew".

"Oss!" The black-belt's cockiness seemed to leave him in one foul swoop.

"Right, students who had good spirit may now leave the dojo. Others grab the cloths and buckets. Dojo no soji!" The class bowed one final bow, some a little more enthusiastically than others.

"You start with a white-belt and end up with a white-belt - you come round full circle"

12

CIRCLE OF LIFE

Uchi Deshi could not help noticing that the Master's black-belt was getting whiter and whiter. In fact you could hardly see any black at all on the much used obi and Uchi Deshi felt that perhaps it would be a nice gesture for the students to purchase a new one for their Master. One that would show the world that he was a much-honoured black-belt, one that wasn't quite so scruffy!

His intentions were all good ones as he entered the Master's office.

"Ah, Deshi San, come and sit down".

"Oss Master", he obeyed quickly, shutting the door quietly behind him.

"I hear a rumour spreading throughout the dojo that you are the instigator in purchasing a new kuro obi for me. Is this true Deshi San?"

"Er, yes Master, how did you find out?"

"Walls have ears Deshi San", he smiled.

"It was supposed to be a secret Master", the young black-belt felt a little dejected to say the least.

"I am only intervening Deshi San to save you time and money. It is indeed a kind gesture, but I would not wear any other belt than the one I have on".

"Why Master?"

"It is the belt I was presented with when I first passed my shodan exam. It is very special to me. Anyway why would I need two. A man only needs one belt to hold up his trousers Deshi San, ne?"

Uchi Deshi smiled and nodded in the affirmative,

"True Master, but it is so white?"

"Ah yes Deshi San and I am a wise old kuro obi, yes?" Again he pulled Uchi Deshi's leg.

"Well, er..... yes Master".

"When your belt is as white as mine Deshi San, then you too will have come round nearly full circle".

"I do not really understand Master?"

"Life is a circle Deshi San. The Earth is round, the Moon is round and all the planets are round, including the Sun. In life we come full circle, from small child to old man or woman. In certain religious burial services it states, 'Ashes to ashes - dust to dust', true Deshi San?"

"Yes Master".

"Even when you walk home from the dojo, you are walking part of a circle, the circle of the Earth. And so it is with your obi. You start with a white belt and you end up with a white belt. You have come full circle. This shows the humility of the true karateka. Some black-belts of high dan grade, have to wear stripes on their belts and badges on their gi, telling the world how senior they are in the art of karate-do. This is hardly the act of a humble man or woman, for at such a level you should have no need to tell anyone how proficient you are, or indeed who you are. On my many travels, I have seen Instructors wearing a badge on their sleeve denoting that they are the 'Sensei'. If outsiders cannot tell who the teacher is, just by the way they conduct themselves, then they must be very insecure karateka indeed. Some yudansha will not be happy until their kuro obi flashes with coloured lights and plays a tune. Can you now see my point Deshi San?"

"Yes I see Master".

"Again Master Funakoshi's words spring to mind, 'Shoshin O Wasurezu', (In your training - do not forget the spirit and humility of a beginner). It is the same with our training, we must always return to basics. Now do you see why I wear an old and battered kuro obi Deshi San?"

"Yes, I do indeed Master".

"Good, then you have learnt an important lesson. We also, as karateka, have a circle around us - the circle of safety".

"How so Master?"

"Come into the dojo and I will explain".

Uchi Deshi bowed and opened the office door for the Master. On his way out the Master picked up a piece of chalk from his desk drawer.

"Right Deshi San, stand in the centre of the dojo".

Uchi Deshi obeyed.

"Now put your right leg out as far as it will stretch, and using your foot as an imaginary marker, slowly draw a circle around yourself".

Again the young shodan obeyed.

As his foot slowly travelled around creating the circle, so the Master followed with the piece of chalk, bringing Uchi Deshi's circle to life.

"Right, now relax in the centre of the circle Deshi San". This he did.

The Master stood just outside of the circle.

"If I were a would-be attacker, what would you do Deshi San?"

The Master took up an aggressive posture.

Uchi Deshi tensed up ready for an imminent attack.

"Relax Deshi San, from here I am no threat to you. I am too far away".

"Oss Master", Uchi Deshi tried to relax.

The Master now moved closer to the edge of the circle. Again Uchi Deshi tensed.

"Relax, I am still not dangerous", the Master's voice was calm and had a relaxing effect on Uchi Deshi.

Then the Master stepped quickly into the circle, menace in his eyes. Uchi Deshi jumped and immediately moved back out of range.

"Excellent Deshi San. You have now moved your circle out of harms way. An attacker is only dangerous once inside your circle, until then stay calm. When he does get aggressive, move your circle away, until the exact moment you are ready to counter-attack. This will always work against an unarmed assailant or an attacker with a knife. Not so good against a gun or bow and arrow!" He smiled at the young student.

"So you see Deshi San, this circle is also of great

importance. It is your circle. Therefore be very careful who you let in".

"Oss Master", he bowed a deep and thankful bow.

"You see the martial arts are a way of life Deshi San, therefore they take a lifetime to understand. Master Funakoshi once stated that, 'You may train for a long, long time, but if you merely move your hands and feet and jump up and down like a puppet, learning karate is not very different from learning to dance. You will never have reached the heart of the matter; you will have failed to grasp the quintessence of karate-do'. So take everything in deeply Deshi San and from today onwards, always remember your circle".

"Oss Master I will, and thank you".

"My pleasure Deshi San, now be off with you. It is time for me to return to the office and complete today's paperwork".

With a final bow Uchi Deshi left the dojo quietly. He had a lot on his mind and could not wait to put the Master's theory to the test the next time he partnered someone for jiyu kumite.

"He told of how one arrow had been enough to kill the great beast"

13

THE TIGER AND THE STONE

Uchi Deshi frowned as he entered the dojo. It was all very different. No longer the shining floor, no longer the empty space where students practised and stretched before the lesson.

Instead the floor was covered with a huge tarpaulin as though the dojo was about to be re-painted. But it had only been thoroughly decorated a few months ago? Strangest of all, there was not a single student in sight. Surely he wasn't that early? And where was the Master? He shook his head in bewilderment, lines appearing on his brow.

All of a sudden the outside door to the dojo flew open. In strode the Master,

"Ah, good morning Deshi San".

"Good morning Master", he bowed, "Where is everyone?"

"Open the door and you will see".

Without further ado he swiftly opened the dojo door

and peered into the street. To his total astonishment twenty or so students stood outside, their arms full of tiles, bricks and pine-boards.

"Hold the door open Deshi San so they may enter".

"Oss Master", again he quickly obeyed.

The students filed in one by one and placed their loads in the centre of the tarpaulin.

The Master could see the bewildered look still emblazoned across Uchi Deshi's young face.

"Do not look so worried Deshi San, we are not building an extension to the dojo", he smiled, "Today is tameshiwari practice!"

Uchi Deshi's eyes lit up. He had always wanted to do this properly. Like most black-belts he had attempted a few 'breaks' in his garden, but nothing like this.

"Why did you not ask me to collect some of the materials Master?"

"You are dojo captain Deshi San, you are excused such duties".

"Oss, thank you Master".

"Thank you is not necessary Deshi San, you have worked extremely hard to attain this position. Now you must stay worthy of such a role".

"I will not let you or the dojo down Master".

"Good, I am glad to hear it. You will be the first to break".

"Oss Master".

The Master walked to the centre of the dojo and started to set up the first stack of tiles to be broken. The tiles were neatly stacked over two large bricks, giving the appearance of a bridge.

Uchi Deshi could not believe his eyes as he slowly counted the tiles the Master had set before him. He quickly recounted. He was right the first time, there were no less than twenty.

"Right Deshi San, prepare yourself to break these tiles".

"Oss Master", his voice slightly quivered.

He slowly strode over to where the mountain of tiles stood and on arrival looked down in total disbelief.

"Carry on when you are ready Deshi San", the Master's voice seemed to take on an effervescent tone.

"Well it's now or never", he thought to himself.

He drew his fist slowly back and made a couple of dummy strikes, sizing up the colossal task ahead. With a powerful kiai his fist fired downwards and smashed into the tiles. He withdrew immediately and looked up at the class confidently.

"Average Deshi San, you have only broken approximately half of the tiles".

He looked down again and to his utter dismay, eight or nine of the tiles lay totally unscathed.

"I am sorry Master, there is no way I can break that many tiles".

"Rubbish Deshi San. You have a strong punch but not such a strong mind. You should be able to break this amount easily. Another twenty tiles! Now try again!"

"Oss Master".

The young shodan obeyed but again he failed, this time leaving at least ten tiles unbroken.

"Sorry Master, I just cannot do it".

"But you can Deshi San. Your mind is making your body weak. All sit down and listen".

The students eagerly gathered round in seiza, forming a circle around their Master.

"There is a very old legend from Okinawa, of a young boy and girl who were very much in love".

The students sat quietly, their minds now captured by the Master's introductory line. He continued.

"One day they were out in the forest walking hand in

hand, when from out of nowhere appeared a huge tiger. The boy panicked and looked for something on the forest floor to defend himself and his loved one with. But all to no avail. The tiger attacked the girl and with one foul swipe of his large razor-like paw killed her outright. The boy was petrified, but as luck had it the tiger ran off back into the forest. Now safely back in his village, the boy mourned for his loved one and vowed to kill the tiger at all costs. His whole purpose in life was to avenge the death of his lost beloved. And so he took up his bow and arrows and strode out into the forest to track the deadly cat. Days passed and nothing. No sign could be seen of the tiger. Then on about the sixth day he saw what looked like the same tiger laying down asleep on the forest floor. Yes, he was sure it was the very same one that had taken his loved one away. He loaded up his bow and took careful aim. He unleashed the arrow. It sped towards its target and penetrated the tiger deeply. The massive cat didn't move a muscle, it was dead. He felt elated as he strode back in triumph to his village. He told of how one arrow was enough to kill the great beast. The villagers were so happy for him and followed the boy back to the kill. On their arrival, the head of the village called the young boy over to the tiger, lying lifeless with the arrow sticking out of its side. 'This is not a tiger, but a striped stone that looks like a tiger'. The villagers and the young boy looked in total disbelief. Sure enough it was exactly as the headman of the village had stated, a large striped stone. The strangest thing though, was that the arrow had deeply penetrated the solid stone. 'He must be an amazing warrior to be able to pierce solid rock with an arrow?' They all chattered excitedly amongst themselves, 'Show us how you did it!' The young boy fired arrow after arrow at the striped rock but every single time the arrows just bounced off harmlessly. 'It is no good, I cannot do it again'. The headman took the boy to one side. 'The reason you cannot now pierce the rock is that your motive is not strong enough. Before you wanted so much to kill the tiger that nothing could get in your way. Your arrows could even pierce solid rock. But now there is no real motive, only to show-off'. With this the boy returned to his village".

The class sat open-mouthed.

"So you see Deshi San, if you really believe in yourself and your motives are honourable, then there is no end to what you can achieve".

"Oss Master".

"Good. Now set up yet another twenty tiles and prepare yourself to break them. Spend some time in mokuso. Think on the task ahead and how you will feel when you have achieved your goal".

"Oss Master", he bowed and set about stacking up the tiles. This done, he knelt by them and meditated. After about a minute he arose a new man. He literally leapt to his feet and confronted the tiles. The class sat in total apprehension, not a sound could be heard. Uchi Deshi sized the tiles up, getting his distance for the immediate task now set and ready before him.

"Haaiiii!" His fist smashed into the tiles with a fearsome force. Bits of masonry flew everywhere. He withdrew and looked from the twenty shattered tiles to his Master, elation beaming from his young face. He bowed deeply.

"Oss Master! And thank you".

The Master returned the bow.

"It is amazing what the body can achieve if we truly believe in ourselves, ne?"

The class 'oss-ed' as one, now dying to have a go themselves.

"This morning Deshi San you have learnt a very powerful lesson. To know others is wisdom, to know yourself is enlightenment".

"Oss! By the way Master, is this where the saying 'Stone-dead' comes from?" An artful smile crept onto his young face.

The Master laughed loudly,

"Very good Deshi San, it is good to have a sense of humour. You may even be right, who knows?"

That day he left the dojo with a deeper knowledge of karate-do and a more positive attitude towards himself and life in general.

❀

*"The fox
is only running
for his dinner,
the rabbit for
his life"*

14

WINTER GASSHUKU

It was deep winter and the snow lay heavy on the Japanese Alps. Each year the Master took the class on a winter gasshuku on the lower slopes of the high mountains. The snow totally covered the peaks of these stone giants but on their lower slopes it was a little more sparse. The trees sparkled in the sunlight and the beautiful sound of water cascading from the many waterfalls was the only sound for miles around.

The class were performing kihon in a small clearing and Uchi Deshi could not help but notice out of the corner of his eye, a fox chasing a rabbit. He was not the only one to spot the two animals dashing through the undergrowth, as many heads turned towards the spectacle.

The Master called, "Yame!"

"Ah, I see you are interested in nature Deshi San, ne?"

"Yes Master, very much so".

"Good I am glad. Who do you think will win that chase Deshi San, the rabbit or the fox?"

"I think the fox Master, it is faster and more cunning". The class generally showed their agreement by the nodding of heads.

"I do not agree", the Master shook his head, "You see the fox is only running for his dinner, the rabbit for his life!" The class watched with baited breath and sure enough the rabbit disappeared down a small hole, leaving the fox frustrated at the entrance.

"Mind you, this is not always the case", the Master continued, "The rabbit must never lose concentration or drop his guard for a second, otherwise he will be caught. Exactly the same applies to our jiyu kumite. A lack of zanshin could be deadly in a real confrontation and the rabbit certainly knows this, for to be caught is certain death".

The class showed their respect by bowing to their wise teacher.

"Right, now partner-up. We shall train in the thick snow, using nature as our matting".

The students quickly obeyed and followed their Master to where the snow lay thick and untouched.

"Right, we shall practice ashi-barai and ukemi for the rest of the morning's session. Find a space quickly".

Again the class bowed and ran to a space in the white snow.

"Deshi San", the Master called the young shodan to his side.

"Class, please watch".

They gathered round.

"Please attack with migi jodan oizuki Deshi San".

Uchi Deshi took up a hidari gedan-barai position.

"Right Deshi San, attack when ready, fast speed".

"Jodan!"

He waited for a brief second and then attacked as fast as he could, his kiai breaking the winter's silence. Before he knew it, he was on his backside. He felt the cold snow slide silently up the sleeves and trousers of his gi. The class looked on in total admiration of the Master's deft sweep and superb mastery of tai-sabaki. Their looks turned to smiles as Uchi Deshi rose slowly and uncertainly to his feet, shaking off the cold snow from his gi.

"Deshi San, you land like a sack of rice. It was a good job it was snow and not hard stone beneath you, ne?"

"Oss Master", he bowed, feeling a little ashamed.

"You must learn to relax as you fall, not tense up on impact", the Master aimed his remark at the whole class.

"Right before we continue, follow me".

The Master led the class over a snow-covered hill and through a small forest. They eventually came upon another clearing. It was one of the most magnificent places that Uchi Deshi had ever seen. At one end was a large waterfall, cascading down into a small clear lake. The rest of the clearing was made up of snow-covered trees and hillocks with winter plants poking up through the soft snow.

The Master made for the waterfall.

"Right, all gather round".

The class quickly obeyed and watched their Master climb on to a small ledge by the waterfall's edge.

Hanging from the ledge were massive icicles, dripping now in the winter sunlight.

"When we are thrown or fall, we must know how to land properly. The body must stay relaxed with the chin tucked in at all times. This will prevent whiplash and damage to the head. If you are thrown to the rear then your forearms and palms must strike the floor simultaneously on both sides of the body. If you are thrown on your side then contact with the ground is made with that shoulder and hip, with only one forearm and palm striking the ground on the contact side. If you are thrown forwards, then you must employ a forward roll, placing your arm, so".

The Master demonstrated the position of the arm.

"These are called, ushiro, yoko and mae ukemi respectively in the martial arts, but also called to-jin-ho in karate".

The class stood and watched attentively.

"Whichever technique you employ, you must relax. Watch what happens to the water as it hits the ground, it runs and floats away naturally. Now watch what happens to ice". He loosed one of the giant icicles. It wobbled and fell, smashing into thousands of fragments on the rock below. "Both are the same element, water. We must be like the water and relax as we hit the ground, not like the ice which shattered on impact. This is the same principal for all our karate techniques. Tension must only accompany the kime of a technique, not the whole".

"How long is kime Master?" A young junior grade had his hand in the air.

"As long as it takes to crush a small bird's egg, no longer. Many students kime for too long. This creates incorrect tension and therefore bad technique. Be like the water, relax and flow".

"Oss!" The class bowed to the Master's superior knowledge.

"Right, back to our clearing and practice. This time we will run back in line. Follow me".

Uchi Deshi could not help noticing how relaxed and lithe the Master looked when he ran. He was truly amazing for his many years.

The class, once back in the clearing, started eagerly practising their ashi-barai and ukemi techniques.

Before long it was time to go home. The weekend had passed all too quickly. Uchi Deshi pondered on the many lessons that he had learnt in the brief weekend in the mountains. It had been a fabulous gasshuku, one that he would remember for the rest of his life and not once had he felt the cold.

15

THE PRODIGY

Uchi Deshi stood quietly by the Master's bed. He had been summoned by the Master to attend that evening's visiting hours. He could not help but notice the pungent smell of disinfectant, akin to all hospitals, as he stood and waited for his Master to awake.

The Master had been taken suddenly ill and rushed to hospital the previous day. It was a minor heart attack and he was to undergo a bypass operation the following morning.

"Ah, Deshi San", he smiled faintly as he opened his eyes. Uchi Deshi could not help noticing how much older the Master looked and it took all of his courage to hold back the tears. Here was the man who had taught him everything, seemingly on the very brink of death.

"Do not grieve Deshi San, I shall be around for a long time yet", again a faint smile appeared on his dry lips.

"I hope so Master, I do not know what the dojo is going to do without you?"

"That is why I have called you here this evening Deshi

San. Tomorrow I have my operation and although I am optimistic about the outcome, I still have to prepare for the worst".

"Oss Master, what is it I can do for you?"

"For the last year or so Deshi San, I have been forging you into, what can only be described as my successor".

"There is no way I could ever become that Master".

"Ah, but you can. Somebody must continue the work I have done. The dojo must survive at all costs, you must see to this personally Deshi San".

"I will try Master".

"Yes I know you will, that is why I have taken a special interest in your training. You are a good young man Deshi San, a credit to me, a credit to the dojo and above all else, a credit to yourself and your family".

"Thank you Master", the young shodan bowed, a lump appeared in his throat, for he knew the Master would never lie.

"No thanks is needed Deshi San, you have worked extremely hard and learnt your lessons well. I have called you here tonight to discuss your new role as Sensei to the dojo. We have a lot of good students of both sexes and all ages, treat them all with equal respect. They are all good karateka, who I know will be willing to learn from you if you treat them fairly. Teach your techniques in depth Deshi San, never just skim the surface".

Uchi Deshi nodded as he listened.

"Remember the saying, 'Give a man a fish and you feed him for a day, teach him how to fish and you feed him for life'. This is an important lesson Deshi San. Always have patience with those who are willing to learn. Patience, Deshi San, is the essential quality of a man and indeed a sensei".

"Oss Master, I understand".

The Master nodded briefly, took a sip of water from his bedside cabinet and continued,

"Create a good and hard-working dojo Deshi San. Remember, 'Atmosphere dominates the attitude'. You must be enthusiastic at all times, even when you do not feel like it, for you now have people's lives in your young hands. Never show-off, only teaching others what you are good at yourself, for it is a great spirit that dares to have a simple style. Admit to your own shortcomings, for a good student will see through you. We are only humans, we all make mistakes, but remember, a sensei is not infallible, but he or she is ALWAYS the sensei. Respect is earned though Deshi San, never demanded".

"Oss Master", again he bowed sincerely.

"I hope to be back in a few weeks Deshi San if all goes well, so until then you will be in sole charge of the dojo. When I do return, you will be my right-hand, my prodigy, my technical embodiment. I will instruct the class, but you will demonstrate some of the more difficult techniques, so keep up your own training during this trying period. Never become just a teacher. For if teaching is the brain, then training is the very heart and soul of karate-do. Both are required for a good sensei Deshi San, ne?"

"Yes Master. I will always train hard in the footsteps of my teacher", he bowed deeply.

"Yes I know Deshi San, that is why I picked you years ago".

"Years, Master?"

"Yes years Deshi San. You had a genuine thirst for knowledge. You asked all the right questions and put the answers in to practice straight away. You are a good student Deshi San, now you must pass on these lessons to others you meet in your life".

"I will try Master".

"Good, now be on your way, I must get some sleep. I have many things to think and pray about before tomorrow".

"Oss Master", he bowed for the last time, "I will ring the hospital tomorrow evening to find out how you are Master".

"Oss and thank you Deshi San, please send my regards to all our students".

"Our students Master? Surely they are all yours?"

"From this moment on Deshi San they become OURS!" He smiled as he closed his eyes and bid his Uchi Deshi farewell.

GLOSSARY

ASHI-BARAI - Foot sweep
ASHI-DACHI - One leg stance.

BASSAI-DAI - Shotokan kata.

DO - The Way.
DOJO - Training hall.
DOJO KUN - Morals of the dojo.
DOJO NO SOJI - Cleaning/scrubbing the dojo floor.
DOMO ARIGATO GOZAIMASU - Thank you (Formal).

FUNAKOṢHI, GICHIN - (1869-1957) Founder of Shotokan karate.

GANKAKU - Shotokan kata.
GASSHUKU - Outdoor training or camp.
GEDAN-BARAI - Lower level sweeping block.
GI - Suit.
GYAKUZUKI - Reverse punch.

HAJIME - Begin or start.
HANGETSU - Shotokan kata.
HANTEI - Decision.
HIDARI - Left.

ICHI - One.

JODAN - Upper level of body.
JIYU KUMITE - Free sparring or free-style.

KAMAITE - Execute or carry out.

KARATE - Empty hand.
KARATE-DO - The way of karate.
KARATEKA - One who practices karate.
KARATE NI SENTE NASHI - There is no first attack in karate.
KATA - Forms or sequences.
KIAI - The shout or cry in the martial arts.
KIHON - Basic or fundamental movements.
KIME - Focus of technique.
KOSHI - Hips.
KUCHI BUSHI - Mouth warrior.
KUMITE - Sparring.
KURO OBI - Black belt.
KYU - Lower grades in the martial arts.

MAE - Front.
MAE-GERI - Front kick.
MAKIWARA - Striking post or pad.
MAWASHI-GERI - Roundhouse kick.
MAWASHI-EMPI-UCHI - Roundhouse elbow strike.
MIGI - Right.
MOKUSO - Meditation.

NAKAYAMA, MASATOSHI - 9th Dan, (1913-87).
NE - Do you understand.
NI - Two.
NIDAN - Second degree black-belt.

OBI - Belt.
OIZUKI - Lunge punch.

OSS - Formal greeting.

SAN - Honourable. A term of respect.
SAN - Three.
SANBON - Three attacks or points.
SEIZA - Japanese sitting position.
SENSEI - Teacher.
SENSEI NI REI - Bow to the teacher.
SHIHAN - Master.
SHIHAN NI REI - Bow to the Master.
SHODAN - First degree black-belt.
SHOSHIN O WASUREZU - Never forget the spirit and humility of a beginner.

TAI-SABAKI - Body shifting.
TAMESHIWARI - Breaking techniques.
TO-JIN-HO - Breakfalls in karate.

TOKUI KATA - Kata of favourite choice.

UCHIDESHI - Private pupil/prodigy/ inside student.
UKEMI - Breakfalls.
URAKEN-UCHI - Backfist strike.
USHIRO - Back or rear.

YAME - Stop.
YIN AND YANG - Two principles in opposition to each other, yet complementary.
YOKO - Side.
YUDANSHA - Holder of black-belt.

ZANSHIN - State of awareness.
ZORI - Sandals.

(Glossary translations are in the context of this book)

DOJO KUN (Morals of the dojo)

HITOTSU! JINKAKU KANSEI NI TSUTOMURU KOTO!
(One! To strive for perfection of character!)

HITOTSU! MAKOTO NO MICHI O MAMORU KOTO!
(One! To defend the paths of truth!)

HITOTSU! DORYOKU NO SEISHIN O YASHINAU KOTO!
(One! To foster the spirit of effort!)

HITOTSU! REIGI O OMONZURU KOTO!
(One! To honour the principles of etiquette!)

HITOTSU! KEKKI NO YU O IMASHIMURU KOTO!
(One! To guard against impetuous courage!)

THE AUTHOR AND ILLUSTRATOR

Malcolm Phipps 5th Dan is the Founder and Chief Instructor of 'Seishinkai Shotokan Karate', a highly respected English karate organisation. He has trained in Shotokan karate now for 20 years, starting in the early 1970's in his home town of Hemel Hempstead with John Van Weenen. On leaving school he served with the R.N. for a period of ten years where he picked up much of the material for his first novel 'Wild Oats in Cornwall', first published in 1992.

He has produced karate champions at all levels of competition, but his first love is traditional karate-do in line with the teachings of Grandmaster Funakoshi.

He has appeared on TV four times in such programmes as; Michael Aspel's 'Six O'Clock Show', Mary Parkinson's 'Afternoon Plus', 'Thames News' with Andrew Gardner and 'Anglia Sport', and was interviewed 'live' on BBC Radio by ex 'Blue Peter' presenter, Simon Groom about his first novel and his karate life.

In 1985 he was voted 'Sports Personality of the Year' for West Herts. He is also joint editor of the karate periodical 'Dojo Magazine', which incidentally was the actual launching pad for the 'Uchi Deshi and the Master' stories.

Tracey Phipps 4th Dan, has trained in Shotokan karate for a period of 14 years and in this time has fought for her Country ten times, taking a total of seven gold medals in these ten outings. In 1983 she was British kumite champion and in 1984 she took the English title at Crystal Palace. 1990 saw her win the FEKO kata title. She retired from competition karate the day she passed her 4th Dan exam in December 1991 with an amazing total of 133 trophies, most of which were won in top class events. She is currently ladies kumite coach to Seishinkai Shotokan Karate and has her own club in Watford. She is also the editor of the childrens section of 'Dojo Magazine'.

In 1982 Tracey was voted 'Sportswoman of the Year' for St. Albans. This is her second book as an illustrator.

Malcolm and Tracey live in Hemel Hempstead with their two Irish Setters, 'Bill and Ben'.